Hello, Family Members,

Learning to read is one of the most important accomplishments of early childhood. **Hello Reader!** books are designed to help children become skilled readers who like to read. Beginning readers learn to read by remembering frequently used words like "the," "is," and "and"; by using phonics skills to decode new words; and by interpreting picture and text clues. These books provide both the stories children enjoy and the structure they need to read fluently and independently. Here are suggestions for helping your child *before*, *during*, and *after* reading:

Before

- Look at the cover and pictures and have your child predict what the story is about.
- Read the story to your child.
- Encourage your child to chime in with familiar words and phrases.
- Echo read with your child by reading a line first and having your child read it after you do.

During

- Have your child think about a word he or she does not recognize right away. Provide hints such as "Let's see if we know the sounds" and "Have we read other words like this one?"
- Encourage your child to use phonics skills to sound out new words.
- Provide the word for your child when more assistance is needed so that he or she does not struggle and the experience of reading with you is a positive one.
- Encourage your child to have fun by reading with a lot of expression . . . like an actor!

After

- Have your child keep lists of interesting and favorite words.
- Encourage your child to read the books over and over again. Have him or her read to brothers, sisters, grandparents, and even teddy bears. Repeated readings develop confidence in young readers.
- Talk about the stories. Ask and answer questions. Share ideas about the funniest and most interesting characters and events in the stories.

I do hope that you and your child enjoy this book.

—Francie Alexander
Reading Specialist,
Scholastic's Instructional Publishing Group

For Alice Bregman, then and now.

*With special thanks
to Marsha Carrington.*

—B.B.

Copyright © 1998 by Barbara Bottner.
All rights reserved. Published by Scholastic Inc.
SCHOLASTIC, HELLO READER! and CARTWHEEL BOOKS and associated logos
are trademarks and/or registered trademarks of Scholastic Inc.

Library of Congress Cataloging-in-Publication Data

Bottner, Barbara.
Two messy friends / by Barbara Bottner.
p. cm.—(Hello reader! Level 2)
"Cartwheel Books."
Summary: Two best friends take on the other's opposite characteristics when they spend the night at each other's house.
ISBN 0-590-63285-X
[1. Orderliness—Fiction. 2. Cleanliness—Fiction. 3. Best friends—Fiction. 4. Sleepovers—Fiction.] I. Title. II. Series.
PZ7.B6586Tw 1998
[E]—dc21
98-21323
CIP
AC

12 11 10 9 8 7 6 5 4 3 2 1   8 9/9 0/0 01 02 03 04

Printed in the U.S.A.   24

First printing, November 1998

Two Messy Friends

by Barbara Bottner

Hello Reader! — Level 2

SCHOLASTIC INC.
New York Toronto London Auckland Sydney

Cartwheel
·B O O K S·®

Grace Marshall is quiet.
I am loud.

Grace Marshall likes to listen to stories.
I like to tell them.

Grace Marshall is neat.

I am messy.

We're best friends
because we're so different.

Friday night, we're having a sleepover.
Mom tells me, "Harriet, you can have
a messy afternoon and a messy evening.
But you can't end up messy."
"No problem, Mom," I say.

Wednesday, I call Grace. "I can't wait until you get here."
"Me, too," she says. "I want to play superheroes and paper chains."
"We can do anything we want," I tell Grace.

On Friday, Grace arrives.
"Let's *go*!" she says and runs
into my room.

Grace wants us to be green superheroes,
so we put green glitter on our cheeks.
We get it on our clothes, too.
But mostly Grace drops it.

At last she says, "I'm tired of this."
She gets the glue to make paper chains.

We make a chain long enough to go around my bedroom. The glue gets all over our fingers, our clothes, and on *my* bedspread.

"I love coming to your house!"
says Grace.

At dinner, Mom tells me to watch how nicely Grace eats.

When Mom's not looking,

Grace draws faces in the spaghetti sauce with her fingers.

After dinner, Grace says,
"Let's take a bath."
And she brings my dolls
and animals into the tub.
"What are you doing?"
I ask her.
"Giving everyone a bath,"
she says.

Grace picks up so many dolls that
they roll down the stairs.
Now the stairs are wet and
everything is messy.

In the morning, Grace and I clean up.
I like cleaning with Grace.
We talk to all my toys and we sing, too.

I don't really mind putting away
my dolls and animals.
But we have trouble getting
the glitter and glue off the floor.

After Grace leaves, I'm so tired.
I fall asleep.

Grace calls me the next day. "When
can I sleep over again?"
"But it's my turn to stay at *your* house,"
I tell her. "How about next Friday?"

When I ask my mother,
she says, "Fine. Please remember
to be as neat as Grace."

At Grace's house, we sing along
to the radio.
I make sure we sing quietly
and in tune.

We have a proper English tea party
with real dishes.
Grace's mother shows us how.

"I am the lady princess," I say. "And,
Grace, you can be the lady-in-waiting."
We don't spill a drop of anything.

Our baths last only six minutes.
"One person at a time," I tell Grace.
I am very strict.

I brush my teeth —
all of them.

We don't have one single
pillow fight. Well, maybe
just a *little* one.

And I count
seventeen clean
white sheep
before I sleep.

"I don't recognize you," says my mother
when she comes to pick me up
in the morning.

"I even *slept* neat,"
I tell her.
"What's your secret?"
she asks.

Grace and I look at each other.

"When you sleep at your best friend's house, you become just like her."

My mother smiles.

Grace's mother sweeps some crumbs off the table.

Then I go home.
Poor Grace!

She has to stay neat.